DEAR LAURA

GEMMA AMOR

GEMMA AMOR   //   ABOMINABLE BOOK

Dear Laura
First Edition July 2019
Cover Illustration By: Gemma Amor

Copyright © 2019 Gemma Amor

ISBN: 9781797875712

For my readers, who held me up, spurred me on, and changed my life.

OTHER BOOKS BY GEMMA AMOR:

CRUEL WORKS OF NATURE

TILL THE SCORE IS PAID

GRIEF IS A FALSE GOD

COMING SOON:

WHITE PINES

Find out more about Gemma's work:
gemmaamorauthor.com

'A guilty conscience needs to confess.

A work of art is a confession.'

Albert Camus

1.

The woman with brown hair walked through the trees in a straight line, her mind's eye fixed on a target. She walked, and checked the compass hanging around her neck after every few steps, travelling as the crow flies, feeling as if she herself were a small, tired, worn-out little bird, doggedly flying north. Migrating to a land she couldn't see yet. It dwelt inside of her, that journey's end. One fixed point. One reason to keep going.

Reddish-brown hair, now threaded with grey and beaded brightly with drops of rain, fell into her eyes, over and over again. Laura was continually forced to push it back from her face with cold fingers, absent-mindedly at first, and then with anger. Her hairband had broken, three miles since. She considered taking out her pocket-knife, hacking the hair off at the roots. But she could not spare the time. Soon, it would be dark. Soon, she would be walking in the forest at night. The darkness did not frighten her. What frightened her was the thought that she would not reach her destination at the designated time. And so she carried on, wiping the hair from her eyes, placing one foot in front of the other, checking the compass that thumped against her chest with each step. All that mattered to her was what lay at the end of the path. Everything else was an inconvenience, only there to be overcome.

Rain fell steadily as she moved through dense undergrowth, high-stepping over weeping fronds of bracken heavy with moisture, snagging her ankles on brambles, stumbling into tree trunks as tiredness gradually took a firm hold of her body. Water worked its way underneath the collar of her jacket and crept into the tops of her boots. Her toes squelched in sodden socks. She kept one hand free as she walked, for balance, and the other jammed hard into her left coat pocket, curled, claw-like, around something.

In that hand rested a crumpled, soggy letter. One of many she had received over the years. She thought this might be the last of them. It was pappy from rainwater, the writing blurred, ink washed away. Unreadable, now. It didn't matter. Every word in that letter was etched into her mind, every single expression, punctuation mark, and errant, elaborate flick of pen on paper that the author was so fond of.

Specifically, there was a code in the letter, or a string of codes, shakily scrawled amongst the self-indulgent ramblings of the man who wrote to her every year, on her birthday. The codes burned into her waking vision, glowing, beckoning, a long sequence of numbers and symbols. She saw them everywhere as she walked: in the trees, in the sky, on the ground, sprouting amongst the ferns like weeds, buzzing around her head like mosquitos.

The others letters she had from the same sender had similar codes in them. She knew what they were. They were directions. And she knew what the letters were. They were admissions of guilt.

Confessions.

I did something terrible, they said.

And that, after all, was why she was here. It didn't matter if the author had a poor grasp of vocabulary, spelling, and grammar. It didn't matter if he was arrogant, and violent, and self-obsessed. It didn't even matter that he was cruel, and had been cruel for so many years, and that she was the primary focus of that cruelty throughout her life.

It only mattered that he had answers.

It only mattered that he knew where Bobby was.

It only mattered that she put an end to it all.

Laura kept on walking.

2.

The first letter arrived on Laura's fourteenth birthday, exactly one year and a day after Bobby disappeared.

She had grown up very quickly in that year. Physically, yes, but in other ways too, more significant ways. By then, she had lost all hope that they would find Bobby alive. Coming to terms with this had a profound effect on the child that she had been, and she sped past the tumultuous awkwardness of puberty like a flat stone flung across the sea. She became, almost overnight, a quiet and serious young woman with a solid grip on the reality of her situation. Her best friend had gone, and he was never coming back. The ties that bind, she realised, did not always bind tight enough. He had slipped from her grasp. And in doing so, he had taught her a lesson, a harsh and immutable truth: that nothing is permanent. Everything can change. A life can alter beyond recognition in the time it takes to simply let go of someone's hand.

His hand in hers was the last thing she remembered about Bobby. She still felt the ghost of his fingers on hers, every day. Hot, smooth, and awkward. Fumbling, stroking her skin. They were clumsy with each other, as teenagers are. She was thirteen, he was fifteen. He had kissed her the day before, on her birthday, lightly on the lips. And now they were 'going steady', as kids said in those days. And going steady meant holding hands.

They had a habit of walking to the bus stop together, and that day, which was also her birthday, had been no different. In matching school uniforms, they dawdled so they could spend more time with each other before the bus arrived. She remembered blushing, stammering as she spoke, unsure of what it was that they were supposed to say to each other now they were boyfriend and girlfriend. They had known each other for what felt like forever- their parents were old, close friends and neighbours- but this felt like new territory, and she was woefully ill-equipped to navigate it. She felt a certain hesitance from Bobby, too, as if he were also unsure as to what the rules were, now that they had begun to explore each other in different ways.

His fingers stroked her hand, and they blushed, and scuffed their feet in shared embarrassment. She wondered if he would try to kiss her again before the bus arrived, but he seemed nervous, his eyes focussed on the road beneath them, so she didn't ask.

And then, she realised she'd forgotten something. What that thing was now, she could barely recall: a pencil-case, her homework, lunch money...it was something small and yet vital, something she would be in trouble for, if she forgot. She let go of his hand.

'I'll just run back,' she'd said.

'I'll be five minutes, wait for me,' she'd said.

She ran up the road, to her house, her bag thumping against her hip heavily, Bobby standing on the pavement, looking into the distance with a small frown on his pale, long face.

She would never hold his hand again.

3.

Thirty years later, Laura was lowering herself carefully down a steep, muddy embankment when her foot rolled, and she fell, heavily, arms flung up uselessly behind her, a wingless bird now, dropping like a stone mid-flight. The impact as she hit the ground at the bottom of the embankment was shattering. All breath left her body. Small sparks of bright crossed her vision, momentarily erasing the code from her sight. There was a sharp, stabbing pain in her ankle.

She lay like that for a little while, trying to suck some air back into her lungs, spread-eagled across a bed of lamb's tongue and bird's nest ferns and moss. The skeletal remains of long-dead trees stuck into her, behaving like old, displeased women, poking her with their sharp fingers, and all she could think was this:

If a woman falls in a forest and no one is around to hear...does she make a sound?

The uncaring rain fell, soaked into the soil next to her face. A rich, thick scent filled her nostrils: the forest, gorged on fresh rainwater, belching out a mulchy, potent aroma as the ground bloated, grew treacherous. She lay there, panting, and tried not to panic about the fading light, about the time slipping away, tried not to think about how much slower she would be now that she was injured, and all the while her ankle throbbed with fierce, shrieking pain, and she sensed that something was very, very wrong down there.

Eventually she regained enough strength to reach down with shaking hands and feel for the problem, the source of the pain. It didn't take long to figure out: instead of flesh, she found a jagged, sharp piece of wood. It was jammed into the soft part of her ankle just above the heel, piercing the gap between her ankle bone and her Achilles tendon, right above her stiff leather boot. Blood, slippery and fresh, flooded down her foot. She wiggled the stick experimentally, and gasped. The pain was incredible, shooting up her entire leg, ricocheting off her back teeth. She knew the piece of wood needed to come out, else she would be crippled and unable to use the leg. And if she was crippled, she wouldn't get to where she needed to be at the right time. Already the day was fading, the tree trunks around her looked less solid, and the sky sank lower to meet the ground. Her window of opportunity was closing inexorably. Time to act.

All obstacles were simply there to be overcome.

Laura clumsily shrugged out of her backpack, freeing up her sore arms. She dug around inside for her small first-aid kit, thankful that she had thought to bring it. There were other things inside the pack: a small trowel, two large bottles of water, a torch, a folded tarpaulin, energy bars, a plastic bag inside of which a bundle of letters lay, bunched tightly together with elastic bands. There was something else at the bottom, too, rolled inside an old towel, something heavy and compact, but she couldn't think about that, now. She scrabbled through the bag's contents and seized the hard green case with a white cross stamped on it, and then, on thinking about it, a bottle of water, and the flashlight. *Basic tenets of first-aid,* she thought, blearily. *Act fast, keep it clean, and apply pressure.* She set the items down carefully on the ground, and then reached for her pocket knife, stashed in her left trouser pocket. She unfolded the blade, switched on the torch, and gripped it between her teeth so that the light shone onto her ankle. It was not yet fully dark, but gloomy enough that she needed the extra beam of light to better see the extent of her injury. The torch revealed a sharp, dry branch from a pine tree, the type that is stripped of bark and comes to a naturally lethal point, like a stake. It stuck out of her skin at an absurd angle, almost jaunty, taunting. Her blood shone bright in the torchlight.

Laura whined and closed her eyes, fighting back nausea. As she did so, a little string of numbers swam beneath her eyelids, teasing her. *You're so close,* they said, excitedly. *Don't give up now!*

She carefully uncapped the lid from the bottle of water and set it to one side. Then she found antiseptic wipes and a wound dressing in the first-aid kit, and set those aside too.

Think of Bobby, she told herself, shrinking from the task at hand.

Bobby.

She leaned forward, gently seized the wood in her right hand, and carefully brought her pocket knife blade to rest against it, intending to lever it away from her ankle if she could not find the strength to yank it out.

Laura counted to ten, chomped down on the torch so hard she thought her teeth would break, squeezed her eyes shut, and *pulled*.

Her screams echoed around the forest, and birds, huddled together in the trees all around, took flight.

4.

When thirteen-year-old Laura returned to the bus stop, Bobby was talking to a man she didn't know through the open window of a dark blue van that was also unfamiliar. Later, she would recognize the model as a Ford Transit, but at the time, it was just a dark blue van parked up on the curb, engine still idling. The man in the driver's seat was talking, and Bobby was listening, and laughing, a little uncomfortable, as young people are when they are humouring adults. Bobby had been brought up well. He was a nice, polite boy. They were from a nice, polite neighbourhood.

He had to stoop, because Bobby was tall for his age, and so all she could see of him was his back, his school bag, and a tuft of his bright blonde hair. She could not see much of the man inside the van, because Bobby was in the way. But she had an idea of the size of him: he was so large, his shadow almost filled the entire front of the vehicle.

Before she could do anything, before she could call out, or catch up to them, the man gestured to Bobby, and opened the passenger side door.

Bobby threw a look at her over his shoulder, a strange, excited expression on his face. In the distance, Laura heard the school bus approach. She raised her hands, shrugging a question at him: *What are you doing?*

Uncertainty glimmered in his eyes. The man in the van gestured to him once more, flapping a huge hand around in a circular 'hurry-up' motion.

Bobby hesitated, and then did something that Laura would never understand.

He jogged around to the passenger side of the van.

And climbed in.

Laura shouted: 'Bobby! What are you doing?!'

The door slammed shut, and Bobby kept his head turned from her, his hair curtaining down to shield her from his vision. A knife slid delicately into her heart as he shut her out, her best friend for years, her companion since babyhood, her new boyfriend of a day. Every morning for the rest of her life she would wake, and find that thin, stinging blade still there, lodged in her chest. If only she could pull it out. If only she could throw away the knife.

But Bobby sat there, in the van, staring at his knees, ignoring her, and Laura saw him mumbling, saw him issue an instruction to the man. Then, the stranger at the wheel of the blue ford transit put his foot down. The van squealed away, belching thick, black smoke from its exhaust. She didn't think to look at the number plate, didn't think to run after, and see where it went. She was a child, and in her world, these sorts of things didn't happen.

The school bus arrived, came to a ponder-ous stop in the road beside her, hissing as the door opened on squeaky hinges. The driver shouted cheerily for her to get in.

The van disappeared from view. Laura was left behind.

And Bobby never came back.

5.

The torment of her ruined ankle was un-
believable. As soon as the stick was out of her flesh,
she felt faint, and the forest spun around her head.
Hot sweat rolled down her face, mingling with the
rainwater. There was so much pain.

Pain is just an obstacle, she told herself eventually, through gritted teeth.

And obstacles are simply there to be overcome.

Jerkily, yanking her hand back repeatedly as
the wound screamed at her, she poured cold, fresh
water from her bottle over her ankle. She wondered
briefly about taking off her boot first, but knew
what would happen if she did: the foot would swell,
and she'd never get it back on. The water rinsed
away fresh gouts of blood and eventually, she could
see a ragged, splinter-flecked wound. She picked out
the splinters as best she could with uncooperative
fingers, and then ran an antiseptic wipe across the
whole mess, before placing a dressing over it and
bandaging the area as tightly as she could without
cutting off the circulation in her foot entire.

That done, she collapsed back against the

floor, exhausted, and thought about giving up. It would so be easy to lie here all night, admit that she was not made of strong enough stuff for this journey. She could drag the tarpaulin she had in her backpack over her body, and sleep until the morning, when she might feel stronger. She could retrace her steps, get herself to a hospital, forget about the letters and the codes, and go back to her life knowing that she tried, at least.

I tried, Bobby. I really did.

But then, the knife would still be there, every day, twisting in her heart, always.

And more than anything, she wanted to wake up and feel safe again. Safe, and whole.

No. She needed to finish this.

'Get up, Laura,' she said, the words swallowed by the incessant patter of the rain. Then, louder:

'Get up.'

And, unbelievably, she did. She packed everything away carefully, tested her balance, ignored the throbbing burn that devoured her leg, and stood up. She checked her compass, and then looked at the folded square of map in a rain-proof case that also hung around her neck. Despite the poor light she was fairly certain she was still roughly on track. Muttering to herself as she calculated her location, she reset her position to compensate for the fall down the embankment, put her injured leg out tentatively, and took a wobbling step forward. Then another, and another.

'I'm coming, Bobby,' she muttered, and the birds in the trees chirruped back softly.

6.

Confrontation was unavoidable, she supposed, a natural by-product of a missing child scen-
ario, but that didn't make it any easier to deal with.
Being the last person to see Bobby alive made quiet,
uncommunicative young Laura a target for other
people's frustration and grief. And Bobby's mother
set her sights on that target early in the aftermath of
her son's disappearance.

She turned up at Laura's house a fortnight
after he had left in the blue van, banging her fists
against the front door in a frenzied manner. Laura
was supposed to be in school, but was instead
curled up in a foetal position on the sofa, a bowl of
popcorn lying untouched by her side, a film playing on the TV that she looked at, but did not see.
Her own mother had taken holiday to be with her.
Mrs Scott did this without complaint at first, but as
the days went by, she became restless. She hovered
anxiously near her daughter, sensing her need but
also finding it a bind. She dropped remarks into
each passing hour about how much extra work she
would have to do as a result of her absence, and the

impact it would have upon her already overloaded schedule. Laura bore these remarks the same way she came to bear all remarks: acknowledging them, shouldering the burden of them stoically, accepting everyone else's discomfort and pain as her own fault, somehow.

And then Bobby's mother came, with her angry fists against the frosted glass of the front door, and before Laura knew what was happening, the distraught, furious woman was inside the house, and through the hall, and into the lounge, and had her hands on Laura's shoulders, and then she was shaking her, hard. Laura's head whipped back and forth, and Bobby's mother, whom she had always politely called Mrs. Eveleigh, despite her insistence that she call her Tara, began screaming at her with a cracked, hoarse voice that belied how many hours of the past few weeks she'd spent crying. She shook Laura like a ragdoll and screamed, and at one point, the slight thirteen-year-old girl thought she might faint.

'How could you let him go like that?' Mrs. Eveleigh shrieked, over and over again. 'You were supposed to be his *friend!*'

Laura bore the assault silently, too shocked to anything else, until her mother raced across the room and wrestled Mrs. Eveleigh away.

'Tara! What are you *doing?*' Mrs. Scott shouted as she held the other woman back, body braced tight as a bow-string against the wind-milling arms and reaching hands that clutched at missing answers. 'What are you doing? She's only a child!

Look at her! Look at her!'

Don't look at me, Laura thought.

Please don't look at me.

And Mrs. Eveleigh stopped, and burst into tears, sagging into her neighbour's arms.

'He's gone, Melanie,' she sobbed, 'my boy, oh, my boy!' Mrs. Scott did her best to soothe her friend whilst keeping her away from her own child.

And Laura lay, discarded on the couch, stunned, head pounding from the motion, and thinking the same thing, over and over, a persistent, nasty thought that echoed like a struck bell:

It's all my fault.

7.

After he was taken, after the fight with Bobby's mother, Laura would wake, each morning, and lie in bed, running the fingers of her left hand along the back of her right hand, mimicking that last moment she'd had with Bobby before he left, trying to recall his face, trying, and always failing. His features had blurred in the year that had passed since that day, and the details bled around the edges like ink on wet writing paper. The knife would twist, and the pain would spread throughout her body.

On the morning of her fourteenth birthday, the day of the first letter, she lay in this fashion, sunlight slicing through her curtains and across the room, motes of dust darting about lazily in the bright, illuminated air. Her fingers caressed the back of her right hand, but the act bought less and less comfort, and so she stopped, and simply held her hands up against the sunlight, studying the outline of her fingers, painted bright gold by the sun. It was while she lay like this that she heard the letterbox snap. She thought no more of it for a moment or two, but then the doorbell rang.

'Go away,' she whispered. The doorbell rang again, and then again, and again, insistent, impossible to ignore. Laura's heart began to thump with irregularity in her chest. She was alone in the house. She often was, despite everything. Her parents drifted across each other's paths like clouds, one arriving home with slumped shoulders and huge, deep circles beneath their eyes just as the other one was heading out to the car. They worked hard to maintain the life they'd built around themselves, forgetting, in the process, what that life was really supposed to be about. It was a lonely way to live, for Laura, but it had always been like that. She'd told herself over the years that it was fine, that she had something her peers did not: as much freedom as she liked. She'd told herself she didn't need her parents hanging around all the time, because she had Bobby.

Except that now, she didn't. She didn't have Bobby. Bobby was gone, and she was alone, on her fourteenth birthday, and someone was at the door, and it frightened her.

The doorbell kept ringing.

Something huge then swelled inside of her. She thought it might have been anger, but she couldn't be sure, because nothing she felt made any real sense to her anymore. The fear burst, like a bubble. She flung aside her duvet, struggled into a shirt, and stomped downstairs, putting the full force of her weight into each step. How dare this person

27

come to her house, and make such a racket? How *dare* they? Why was everything so bloody *unfair?*

She slowed as she reached the bottom, and looked to the front door. She could see a dim shadow behind the frosted glass, dark, and tall. Too tall and broad to be a woman. She hesitated. She could see a pile of bills and other letters sitting on the doormat. The postman had already been, that day. Whoever this was, it was not the postman. But it *was* a man, a big, tall man, in dark clothing.

Laura's anger melted away. She was alone in the house, and her best friend had been taken from her by another such man, a big man like this, a face-less mystery man. She held her breath, not wishing the person to know she was there after all. Sus-picion had become part of her natural chemistry. Every stranger was the bogeyman. There was dan-ger, now, around every corner.

Too late, Laura realised with a sudden, sick jolt that the man could probably still see her stand-ing there in the hall through the frosted glass, every bit as well as she could see him standing out there in the porch. Despite this, she remained motionless, rooted to the spot, waiting.

The doorbell rang once more, and she flinched, but kept her distance.

Then, slowly, her letterbox opened.

She thought with horror that she would see an eye, rheumy and frantic, staring into her house through the small slit in the door. Or a hand, finger-nails dirty and broken and bloodstained, reaching for her. She saw neither. Instead, a thin, yellowish envelope slid through and landed onto the mat with a soft noise. She did see the tips of thick, red fingers for a brief flash. Then the flap snapped down. Moments later, the dark shadow straightened, then moved away from the glass.

She waited a further fifteen minutes, breathing hard, tingling from head to toe, until she was sure she was safe. Then, she moved forward, bent down carefully, and picked up the letter as if she were picking up a dirty rag, holding it away from her body, pinched tight between her thumb and forefinger.

The envelope was handwritten. No postage stamp. Definitely not the postman, if she'd been in any doubt. The postman didn't deliver mail without postage stamps.

It was addressed to her, one word written in a strongly slanted hand, the ink pressed hard into the soft, dirty ochre of the envelope, an intimate word. The most intimate.

Her name.

Laura, it said, confident, over-familiar. No 'To,' or 'For the attention of,' or surname.

Just her name.

It felt wrong. The letter felt wrong in her hands. She'd mistaken it for a birthday card, that would make sense, today being that day, but this was thin, and lightweight. It was a letter. A handwritten letter.

Made out to her.

She opened it.

8.

The forest leaned in on the woman that had once been the child, and she limped on stubbornly beneath a canopy of dripping leaves. She knew that walking on her leg was a bad idea. She knew, and carried on anyway. Every step she made pressed her wound painfully against the unresisting leather of her boot, and as early evening gradually became the first, tentative flush of twilight, it became harder for her to find a steady footing on the uneven forest floor. She stumbled repeatedly, root snarls and barbed loops of blackberry bushes lurking everywhere, and wondered why it was that she couldn't cry, like normal people. Had she in fact died, years ago? Was she now just a ghost, a memory of a girl in pain, drifting, endlessly drifting, towards something indistinct?

There were no answers from the trees, only more roots, more discomfort.

The rain gradually petered out. The air grew quiet, and hung heavy, laden with scent. Colours slowly leached away as she moved, and she found herself hemmed in by shadows, by muted greys and browns, by pockets of dark. Time was running out. A mounting anxiety started to eat away at her resolve.

What if she got lost?

What if she didn't make it in time?

What if...

Don't, she told herself, unhooking her trousers from another bramble, feeling the fabric snag and tear like the fabric of a thirteen-year-old girl's heart.

But what if? This particular question would not be dislodged from her mind, no matter how hard she tried to reason with herself.

What if there was no Bobby at the end of this rainbow?

What if the person she was supposed to meet didn't show?

She stopped, overwhelmed by a squeezing fist of dread, and doubt.

What if he did?

And what if, because of that, she died out here, alone in the forest?

The trees bowed their heads, whispering gently.

Don't stop, they said.

She walked.

9.

The letter was written in a heavily angled hand that was hard to read. Laura skimmed each sentence, frowning, and then re-read more slowly, lips moving as she spoke the words out loud, something she only did when trying to solve a hard equation in her maths homework.

As she read, her heart sank to the bottom of her belly, and the words began to rattle around inside her brain. And once they were there, there was no getting them out. She was stuck with them, for life. Little, poisoned words.

Dear Laura,

You don't know me yet, but I know you. I've been watching you. I know you, and I know your friend Bobby.

I know where Bobby is.

Laura put a hand to her mouth. The letter continued:

Bobby is dead.

She read this, and felt a peculiar rushing sensation in her ears. Her heart contracted in her chest so hard she thought she might die right there on the spot. She reached out blindly for the stair bannister behind her, and slowly felt for the bottom step, upon which she collapsed, knees splayed out, frog-like. Her eyes stung, but remained dry. All the tears she was supposed to cry were trapped in the cavity around her heart, and they would stay there for many years to come, solidifying to a hard, waxen case.

> *I'm sorry for it.*
> *I couldn't help it.*
> *I expect you'd like me to tell you where he is. I expect you think I'll do it out of the goodness of my heart, or because I feel guilty. I am sorry for what I did. But I don't trust you well enough yet to tell you my secrets, not yet. You have to earn my trust.*
> *So here's how it works, Laura. If you want Bobby, you have to give me something first. Something personal. If you do as I ask, I will send you a clue. Something for something, an eye for an eye, all natural and fair, just like nature intended. Do you see? It has to be fair. That's the rule. Like a game. I know you like games, Laura. I watch you playing them sometimes with your family.*
> *I think you are very beautiful, Laura. Has anyone told you that, yet? I hope not. I would like to be the first to say it. You are beautiful. Sometimes I watch you and all I can think about after is your sweet face.*
> *There is another rule I must tell you about.*

This one is easy. If you take this letter to the Police you will never find Bobby's body. This has to be our secret, or the arrangement is off.

No Police. I hope I can trust you, Laura. I shall send further instructions separately.

Yours with respect,

X.

10.

Once the dark had turned its gaze on the forest, there was no stopping it. Soon Laura was surrounded by the full force of the night, and moving on became impossible. Every space grew treacherous, every surface unreliable. It was summer, so dawn would not be that far away, but she was afraid she had no time to wait for it. She was supposed to be at her destination by seven-thirty the next morning. *Seven-thirty, or I will come after your boy, and I will take him like I took Bobby,* the last letter had said.

Eventually, the decision was taken out of her hands. It was too black a night for her to reliably keep to the straight line she had plotted on her map. Every misstep she took in the dark jolted her swollen, tender ankle and brought her immense discomfort. When she walked into a low-hanging tree branch, spearing herself on another pointed twig and narrowly missing an eye in the process, she admitted defeat.

Sometimes, all you could do was give in. Sometimes, you just had to let the night win. *Lose the battle, win the war,* she thought to herself, and the heavy, towel-wrapped bundle in her backpack felt a lighter, suddenly.

11.

Three days after Laura's fourteenth birthday and her first letter, one year and four days after Bobby Eveleigh disappeared, Mr. and Mrs. Eveleigh gave into public pressure, and held a memorial service for him. Technically, Bobby was still listed as missing on the police files, his case marked unsolved. There was no public acknowledgement that anyone thought Bobby was dead, and no explicit mention of foul play. But the Eveleighs held a service, anyway. It would become an annual tradition, something concrete for them to do as they waited in vain for their golden boy to return.

Despite there being no body, no burial, and no specific mention of the word 'death', the service still had all the uncomfortable, itchy trappings of a funeral. It was held on a Sunday in the local church, and there were candles, poems, large framed photographs of Bobby wreathed with flowers and football memorabilia. His smile echoed around the congregation, all of whom wore black. Laura stood alone at the back of the church, her own parents absent because of work commitments, and she felt hatred for the first time in her short life, hatred for Bobby's mother and father and little brother, pure, white hot rage, rage that burned through every filament of her being, because this service was an admission of only one thing: that everyone else was giving up on Bobby.

She vowed then, as she looked about the church and saw other pupils from her school holding hands and crying, boys and girls who had never spoken to Bobby in their lives, who never knew him at all, she vowed, as she took in the smirk of a small boy from four houses along who was pulling a funny face at his sister, bored, she vowed, as she let her eyes settle for a moment on the careful, neutral expression of the church vicar as he delivered the Lord's Prayer, she vowed, as she clutched a printed hymn sheet with white-knuckled hands and screamed internally, that she would go along with the letters. She would do whatever the mystery man wanted, if it meant that she could find answers to it all. She was not too young to understand what closure meant. She was not too young to feel the agony of not-knowing.

She crept away before the service ended, wanting to avoid all the other attendees. As she left, she glanced backwards into the church, and met the eyes of Tara Eveleigh, who was watching her leave. Her gaze was dark and dangerous, and her tears bright on her cheeks.

Laura felt the burden of that stare all the way home, where she found another dirty envelope, waiting for her on the doormat.

She opened it, and read the following words:

Underwear, it said.

One pair of your panties.

Not clean ones. Used panties, folded up in a plastic bag.

Leave them on your doorstep tomorrow morning, behind the small tree in the pot.

When this is done, I will give you your first clue.

I want to be able to trust you, Laura.

Yours with respect,

X

12.

Confused, she put the letter down, and walked away from it, feeling sick to her stomach, the skin on the back of her neck prickling as if someone were breathing on it from behind.

No way, she thought, red spots of embarrassment pooling on her cheeks.

No way.

Humiliated, and deeply disturbed, Laura found herself with a decision to make. The letter had said no Police, but what she was being asked to do was wrong, and she knew it. The next step should be to inform an adult. The next step should be to throw the letter away, burn it, and forget it ever happened.

But then what about Bobby?

The child that she still was wanted desperately to fix everything, to bring him back, and this letter might be her chance.

And really, what did she care about a pair of old knickers, when it came down to it? If she could just give Mrs. Eveleigh some answers, maybe she wouldn't hate her as much as she did, or continue to blame her for Bobby's disappearance. It never occurred to Laura that it was unfair of Mrs. Eveleigh to blame a teenage girl for something as profound and terrible as the loss of her son.

Crushed by the weight of responsibility, and exhausted by the idea that even if she told her parents what was happening, they might not believe her, or take it seriously, Laura's resistance crumbled.

She did as she was told.

She went upstairs to the bathroom laundry basket and pulled out one pair of her plain cotton knickers. She found a plastic bag and folded them up inside, a hot, lurching, urgent feeling in the pit of her tummy. Then, she tucked the plastic bag behind the small potted bay tree by her front door.

Afterwards, she hid in her room, ashamed and terrified of what she had just set in motion, knees drawn up to her chest, a pillow over her head, held there until she almost suffocated herself, a useless, pathetic shield against the bogeyman lurking outside her front door.

Eventually, she decided to check the letterbox, in case her mother came home from work and stumbled across something she shouldn't. She extricated herself from her cocoon and crept downstairs, opening the front door a tiny, barely perceptible crack.

The bag was gone. In its place, there was another envelope. Inside *that* was a scrap of paper, and on it, the first clue:

φ 50.9025. Λ -1.63403114

Which made absolutely no sense to her whatsoever.

After this, he had written one standalone sentence, and it was this that confused her most of all:

I loved him, you know.
Yours with respect,
X.

This would have been a good point for Laura to have burst into tears. But she didn't. She took the letter back upstairs, and pinned it on her notice-board, where she could lie in bed and look at it. The numbers, after an hour or so of staring at them without comprehension, burned into her brain, committed indelibly to memory.

She slept, and digits danced around her as she stood, alone, in a candlelit church, the sound of Mrs. Eveleigh's weeping rising and falling like the tide all around her.

13.

After the first clue, there was nothing. No more letters, no more codes. She waited, heart constantly in her throat, so that she felt as if she were always swallowing, always massaging her neck to get her heart back into the right place, sure that any day now there would be another letter, another request, another clue, another tit-for-tat. She waited, and disappointment became another rock to carry, a rock painted a different colour, but a rock the same size and weight as the rocks she already bore: those smeared with the colours of guilt, and grief, and shame.

She could not stand the thought that she had been fooled into sending underwear to a mysterious pervert taking advantage of Bobby's disappearance. Laura held a thin belief that people were inherently good, not evil, although that belief was eroding quickly. So, she waited, but her patience was met with one thing: a resounding silence.

Still, she had the code, and that was better than nothing. She quickly figured out that the code was a geographical location, a latitude and longitude. According to an old map she found in her father's study, it pointed to a spot in the middle of a road that ran through a part of the vast, sprawling Old Forest only twenty miles away. From that point on, she became convinced that this was where Bobby's body was buried. It consumed her every waking thought, that one, single location. It dragged her out of her grief, and threw her into action.

She got a job delivering papers, worked hard every day, saved her money, bought a compass, bought a brand new ordnance survey map from the local tourist information office, took a bus, then walked to the exact spot in the Old Forest that the coordinates pinpointed.

And found herself standing by a quiet roadside next to a car park on a place called Stoney Plain. To either side of her, there was scrubland, ringed by the huge, far-reaching mass of woodland that stretched far into the horizon and beyond. Behind her, there was more road, leading back the way she'd walked. In front of her, a dual carriageway bisected the horizon, bracketed by cattle grids meant to stop livestock and ponies from wandering into traffic. Aside from a dog-walker mooching along in the distance, she was alone, and she cut a forlorn, thin figure as she dithered on the roadside.

It had taken all her energy to get to this point, and now she was here, she didn't really know what to do. She scanned the ground to either side of the road, couldn't see anything that looked obvious, like a grave or a trench, and then sat down wearily on the scrubby verge.

What am I doing here? She thought blindly, head in her hands. And then, the last words in the last letter, the words that kept her up at night, raced through her mind:

I loved him, you know.

Moments later, she gave in to the realisation that Bobby wasn't here, after all, and that she was on a wild goose chase, and embarrassment and shame landed heavily on her.

The dog walker shuffled past as she sat there, a picture of misery. He was accompanied by a large black and white collie dog on a lead. He stopped, eyeing her curiously.

'You alright, miss?' He said, stooping so that she could better hear him. The man was large, and tall, very tall, and very broad, but Laura didn't register this, didn't even look up. If she had, something in her memory might have been triggered.

Instead, she hid her eyes behind her hands and refused to answer, furious at the intrusion.

The man waited, wrestling with himself internally, then spat into the verge.

'Suit yourself,' he said, and shuffled off, the dog trotting at his heels obediently. If Laura had been watching, she might have noticed the man's reluctance to leave. If Laura had been paying attention, she might have seen that he held an envelope in his free hand, a dirty, yellow envelope very similar to the type she received on her birthday, and she might have seen that he wore a strange, excited smirk on his face, too.

But Laura wasn't paying attention to anything except her own predicament. And eventually, she realised she couldn't stay out here for the rest of the day, so she retraced her steps, got back on the bus, and arrived home to an empty house with all the lights off. Drifting upstairs, pale, and weary, she collapsed on her bed, and didn't move from there for three days.

Eventually, Mrs. Scott realised that all was not well with her daughter, realised that she was, in fact, not eating, not drinking, and not going to school. She sat on Laura's bed on the morning of the fourth day, registered the pallid, drawn face, the thin, ghostly limbs, and the hollow, sunken eyes. She realised with a burgeoning sense of sorrow that this was confirmation of something she had long been trying to ignore: that her daughter, despite all outward appearances of resilience and strength, was really not okay.

She put in a request to reduce her hours at work, and then took Laura to see a Doctor. The Doctor loosely diagnosed her with nervous exhaustion, and wrote a prescription for some pills with a long name that Laura couldn't remember. Laura took the pills for a week, and then started flushing them down the toilet. If anything, they made her feel even more numb than she already did, coating her thoughts in an unpleasant layer of fuzz.

The silence from X continued.

After a time, Laura learned not to wait for the snap of the letter box in the morning. It became painfully apparent to her that she had been the butt of a particularly cruel joke. She continued to grow, in both height and pain, and the memory of Bobby's face softened further, until he became like a smudged finger-painting in her mind, and she blamed herself for forgetting him like this, because she considered it her duty to remember him when everyone else was apparently moving on.

And then, her fifteenth birthday dawned. And, finally, after a year of radio silence, nestled in amongst the birthday cards on the doormat, she found the letter she'd been waiting for.

Dear Laura, it said, and her teeth began to hurt.
Did you miss me?

14.

In the forest, once Laura resigned herself to sleep, it came quickly. There was little point in fighting the dark: it comes for everyone, in the end. Better to accept this, and work harder when the light returned. Laura bundled herself into a small, aching ball at the base of a rhododendron bush, wrapped a tinfoil survival sheet around her shoulders for extra warmth, and closed her eyes.

In no time at all, the alarm on her watch was beeping, and Laura awoke. Dawn was already ahead of her, spreading its pale fingers through the fronds of ferns, nudging awake the birds in the trees all around. A squirrel leapt from one limb to another above her head, chuckling away to itself as it did so. A small shower of pine needles accompanied him, drifting onto her head, where they remained, for she was too tired to brush them away.

She knew almost immediately after waking that there was something wrong with her body: it was wracked with a feverish type of shuddering that she just couldn't seem to control, like a palsy. She added this new discovery to her pile of inconveniences. *How many more obstacles can there be?* She said to herself, woozily, cramming an energy bar into her mouth to try and quell the shakes. She followed this up with a handful of paracetamol from her first-aid kit, and washed it all down with water that was still refreshingly cold, somehow. She had to tip her head back a ways to get to it: there wasn't much left, but she didn't plan on being out in the forest for much longer. She checked her watch. Four-forty-five in the morning. She needed to be where she needed to be by seven-thirty. She calculated that she had just under three hours to travel another five miles, which should be more than achievable. She thought that, and then she stood up.

Once again, her screams echoed around the forest.

15.

Dear Laura,

Did you miss me? I missed you. You are never far from my thoughts, you and Bobby. There are so many things I want to say to you, but I am afraid to out of fear for what might happen to me. I could get into trouble for writing letters to a fifteen year old girl. Society judges people with feelings like mine.

I'm not keen on the way you wear your hair these days, Laura. And the make-up is not good on you either, if you don't mind me saying so. You're a beautiful young girl. Don't try to look older than you are.

Are we learning to trust each other yet, do you think? I keep your gift close by at all times, even when I sleep. I can smell you on them.

I wasn't lying with my earlier letters, or playing a cruel trick. I want to give you another clue. But, you have to pay me first, that's how we make things fair.

I want your (used) toothbrush, wrapped up in the usual place.

Yours faithfully, and Happy Birthday,
X

16.

The letters came like clockwork after that, once a year, on her birthday. Clues piled up, locations, symbols, possible places that Bobby could be.

Every year X demanded something else of hers in exchange for these clues, something she had used: a lock of her hair, her favourite t-shirt, a piece of paper with a lipstick kiss on it, even a dirty sanitary pad. She gave him these things wearily, having been conditioned to obey, thinking with every letter that she would go to the Police, and then telling herself that doing so would jeopardise the only real connection she still had with Bobby. She parcelled everything her pen pal wanted up in plastic bags, tucking it into the space behind the tree in the terracotta pot by her front door, and each year he sent her a new set of coordinates in return for her offering. *Something, for something,* he'd said.

She learned to approach everything else in life this way: *quid pro quo, I'll do this, if you do that.* It stretched her already fraught relationship with her mother to something papery, thin, and brittle. She would only obey instructions if she was first given something to make the sacrifice seem worthwhile. Even the smallest of daily tasks became a negotiation: 'I'll only go to school,' she said once, over breakfast, 'If you pay for my driving lessons.' The statement dropped into the silence between them like a concrete weight, and her parents looked at each other, knowing better by then than to argue. Instead, they gave Laura what she wanted, and she was driving before the year was out. She continued at school, excelled in class, passed all her exams with flying colours. Her behaviour in all other respects was faultless: she never acted out, or drank, or partied. Laura kept herself to herself, and gave nothing to anyone without first accepting payment. It broke her mother's heart, but by the time Laura was eighteen years old, the damage was done, and Mrs. Scott didn't know how to go back in time and repair the cracks in her child. She considered herself lucky that Laura hadn't given into drugs, or gone off with an unsuitable man, and all the time, Laura kept wrapping little, intimate parts of herself up in plastic, and leaving them outside her front door, like donations to a perverted god.

As the latitude and longitude codes came in, year after year, she marked them on her map, and then took that map, her compass, and enough money for the bus fare until she passed her test and got her driver's licence, and went on excursions. Each time she ended up somewhere innocuous and not remotely momentous, to a spot where Bobby couldn't possibly be buried: the very middle of a busy road, or next to a public phone box, or in a random car park. Once, she even stood dead in the middle of a frozen food aisle in a supermarket, map in hand, foolishly staring at the rows of cabinets stocked with ice cream and frigid chopped vegetables. Shoppers gave her a wide berth, eyeing her nervously, but she had learned long ago to avoid the judging eyes of others, and instead created her own sad little bubble of stillness in the aisle around which everyone else flowed like water around a stone.

After that, something changed inside of her. The fragile hope she'd nurtured that this was all leading somewhere began to sour, and curdle. She began to ask herself difficult questions as she lay awake in bed at night, staring at her hands in the gloom, numbers trickling past her wide open eyes like drops of rain down a window pane. Questions she didn't know how to ask herself when she was thirteen.

Was the man who wrote the letters *really* the same man that had driven away with Bobby?

Did she actually believe that the end result of this sordid letter-writing campaign would lead her to the remains of her dead best friend? Or had she pushed herself to believe it so that she could make peace with her own complicity? And, whether or not they were the same person, who was the man in the blue van, really? Why had Bobby been talking to him? Did Bobby know him from somewhere, already? Was Bobby's awkwardness with her that day related, somehow? He had only kissed her once, and not shown any signs of wanting to repeat the kiss. Was this because of his age, his inexperience?

Or was it because...had he discovered that kissing girls was not for him, after all? Did he prefer kissing men? Older men?

She remembered him leaning into the car, laughing. She remembered how he hid his face behind his hair when he climbed into the van. Had he been ashamed? Embarrassed?

Had Bobby been taken?

Or had he, in fact, run away?

And if so, why had Bobby chosen the stranger, over her?

Other questions began to plague the restless hours she spent trying, and failing, to sleep at night. Could she take the letters to the Police, now, all these years later? What would they think of her when she told them about the underwear, the sanitary pad? What would they be able to do about them, realistically? She knew little of DNA, but she knew something of evidence. What evidence was there, really, in the letters? Evidence to prove that Bobby was actually dead, evidence to prove definitively that her mysterious pen pal really knew where Bobby's body was? Simple: there was none. All she ever got were demands. All she ever got were map coordinates. The man was a crackpot, and she was indulging him, a willing participant in an elaborate prank. The Police would never take her seriously. The letters would be lost, filed away in a box folder in a storage room somewhere, and she would lose her only slim chance of finding a resolution.

But, a little voice warned, periodically. *But.*

It might not be a hoax. Her writer friend might be crazy, might be a pervert, but he *might* also be telling the truth. She might not have debased herself for nothing. Maybe she *was* building trust, like an undercover agent, or mole, and at the end of the process, there would be answers for everyone who once loved Bobby, herself included.

And she couldn't risk throwing that away, no matter how improbable it seemed.

She grew older, and the questions remained unanswered. The curdled sour-milk abscess in her core split open, and the tough outer skin peeled back, flooded her system with bile, and impotent, slow anger. She swallowed it down and retreated further into herself, aware that the people around her in life did not have the very first clue as to how to talk to her about what she was experiencing.

And the memory of Bobby drifted further, and further away.

Eventually, as she approached her nineteenth year, fatigue won out: she decided that she didn't want to play, anymore. She decided to cut ties with everything that defined and imprisoned her, and leave home. Bobby wasn't coming back, that much was obvious, now, and she had finally, finally grown weary of the game, especially after the supermarket prank. Age had given her some resilience when it came to accepting that Bobby was gone for good, and she no longer felt the loss as keenly as she had when she was thirteen. It coloured her life in dull shades, but didn't blind her completely to the other opportunities there were out there for her, if she could just move on.

And so move on, she did.

Or at least, she tried to.

Before she left, early on the morning of her nineteenth birthday, she woke with the dawn, deliberately. She wanted to be up and about before X had time to slip his noxious little envelope through the letterbox. She sat at her small desk and wrote her own letter on pristine white notepaper, then left it wrapped in a plastic carrier bag behind the bay tree. It was short, and to the point:

Dear X,

Who the fuck are you, anyway? Why are you doing this to me? You don't know where Bobby is at all. I think you're a pathetic, dirty old man who is sick in the head.

You are disgusting.

I don't want to play, anymore.

Leave me alone.

L

Having committed this small, revolutionary act, she used it as fuel to find a place of her own, and find one, she did, that very day- a small studio flat in the centre of town, above a convenience store. It was pokey, and damp in places, but she could afford to pay the deposit and first month's rent with her meagre savings, and affordability was the main criteria.

And just like that, she flew the nest. She got a job in a supermarket stacking shelves in the dead of night, even, in time, found herself a new boyfriend, although their relationship was extremely loose and casual, because Laura didn't know how to trust, and certainly didn't know how to let anyone close to her.

Regardless, life became less jagged around the edges. She walked with a straighter back, and her face became softer, more open. Friends soon followed, friends who took her on shopping excursions, and sat on lunch breaks with her in the sun, reading magazines and rolling cigarettes and doing normal, everyday things, things Laura had denied herself for years, so preoccupied as she'd been with finding Bobby. Laura hadn't made any friends in school after Bobby left, and the extended loneliness she'd experienced made her grateful for every new relationship she now forged. She even made some inroads with her mother, inviting her over for a meal a time or two, although never her father: that road was potholed beyond repair.

Life improved, and she was allowed to live like this for twelve months. During that time, she convinced herself that X had taken the hint, given up, moved on. Perhaps she'd scared him away with her own letter. Perhaps it had been a wake-up call: she was onto him. Perhaps he had grown equally as tired of the game as she had. A beautiful silence reigned, and breathing became easier, every day that passed. Her birthday approached, and she thought, finally, that this one might pass with no yellow envelope.

I won, she thought. *All I had to do was stop playing.*

But she was wrong.

17.

Twelve months. Another year travelling around the sun.

No yellow envelope.

Heart singing, she went to work, and ate the cheap sponge cake her colleagues had bought to mark the occasion. The shift passed quickly, and she returned home at four in the morning, looking forward to a good sleep.

Looking forward to the rest of her life.

Until she found her bathroom window shattered, and glass all over the floor.

Lying amongst the splinters, she found a brick. Attached to the brick with gaffer tape was an envelope. Same yellowish paper, same slanted, angry writing. Presumably, the same word vomit on the same cruel, malignant subject matter.

How had he found her?

She stared at the mess in silence, then boarded up the broken window as best she could with a sheet of cardboard, and went to bed, leaving the envelope where it was, taped to the brick on the floor.

Her dreams were dark, and endless.

When she woke, she thought about throwing the letter away, unread, or better still, burning it. But she didn't. Whether from guilt at her short-lived happiness and peace, or addiction, or from being conditioned by him over the years to receive his instructions, regardless: she found herself sitting on the closed lid of her toilet, finger sliding beneath the grubby, saliva-rippled envelope flap, and inside, there was no letter, only a photograph.

No. Two photographs.

The first was of Bobby, of course it was. Fresh faced, wearing the school uniform he'd been wearing the day he disappeared. His hair, in long blonde curtains, was tucked back behind his ears, a style she'd never seen on him before, and she'd known him since he was a baby. He was smiling hesitantly into the camera, although the smile looked brittle, forced. He had his arm around someone, an older man, a large man with huge shoulders and a dark blue t-shirt, a man she presumed was X. She couldn't see his face, because he had cut it out of the photo, leaving behind a precise little hole through which she could poke her index finger.

On the bottom right of the photo a digital readout was stamped in orange type: the time and date it was taken. The same day that Bobby had disappeared. Five hours, in fact, after she'd seen him drive off in the van.

She slipped the second photo out from behind the first with her thumb, and screamed.

Bobby wasn't smiling anymore. His eyes were rolled back in his head, unseeing.

And the rest was all red.

Red.

So.

Much.

Red.

She stared. Her hands shook. She gently laid the photograph on the bathroom floor, and hung her head between her knees, trembling.

This was the proof that she had been lacking.

Her brain ticked over like an over-heated engine, straining to work through the implications of this image, and two things swam to her, slowly:

X knew where she lived, which meant he was following her, stalking her. He hadn't grown bored of the game. He hadn't given up.

And this...

This picture was evidence.

And Bobby was dead.

Really, truly, without a doubt, dead.

X knew where the body was. The letters were, after all, confessions, and not just crazy ramblings.

Laura felt her stomach cramp, felt something hot surge up from inside. She kicked the photos to one side and vomited onto the bathroom floor. The sickness was a replacement for tears: instead of crying, she evacuated her stomach and then panicked, cursing herself for almost destroying the only piece of evidence she had proving Bobby's fate.

On autopilot, she carefully retrieved the pictures, and checked to see if they were damaged whilst trying not to look at the images within. Then she wiped her face with a tissue and made her way unsteadily to her bedroom, where she raided her drawers for all the other letters she'd kept over the years. Despite everything, she'd never been able to bring herself to throw them away, feeling somehow that the letters were an unpleasant but vital part of her, and not something she could dispose of lightly.

She collected them into a bundle, stuffed everything into a handbag, jammed her shoes onto her feet, and started walking to the Police station.

The whole way there, all she could see was red.

I made a mistake, she thought, miserably.

Bobby is dead.

I made a mistake.

This is all my fault.

She recalled with horror how she hadn't taken the letters to the Police out of fear. Fear that she wouldn't be believed. Fear that she'd been tricked. So much time, wasted. And here she was, years later, with a definitive, unspeakable answer to the question of what had happened to Bobby. Answers for Mr. and Mrs. Eveleigh. How much more would they hate her now? More than they already did? Was that even possible?

Oh, Bobby. So much red in your hair.

She was only two streets away from the station when she heard heavy footsteps running close behind her. She turned, but too late: a huge hand clamped over her eyes. Her feet were kicked out from beneath her. She fell to the ground, and knew, suddenly, what was happening: she'd been followed.

By X.

Her handbag, containing the letters and the photos, was ripped from her shoulder. A tall, dark presence loomed over her. The hand over her eyes disappeared. As she blinked, it reappeared once again, only this time it was a fist, and it hit her squarely in the centre of her nose. Something cracked, and the heavy feet thumped away. The man, his fist, her handbag, the letters, and the photos were all gone.

The evidence had been confiscated.

She'd broken the rules of the game.

She was helped to her feet by a small crowd of passers-by. Several of them offered to come with her to the Police Station to report the attack. She shook her head, squirmed awkwardly out from beneath the grip of their anxious, hot hands. Blood dripped out of her nose and splattered onto the pavement. Concerned faces crowded in all around her. She pushed them away, swearing, and hobbled home, keeping her head back and pinching her nose to stem the blood flow. People called out behind her. She picked up her pace and ran, away from the voices, away from her blood on the pavement, away from her shame.

A day later, before she could fix the broken window in her bathroom, her letters, and her handbag, were returned. Not left outside her door, not this time.

No. He left the bag at the foot of her bed, with a note, while she slept.

As expected, the photographs were gone.

The note read:

No Police.
Yours respectfully
X.

18.

She was certain her nose was broken, but she didn't go to the Doctor. Her fear of the outside world, where X lurked in the shadows, held her prisoner. The memory of the photos filed every space in her brain, and the idea that X had been inside her house, this time, walked into her bedroom while she slept, spurred her into a frenzy of activity. She pulled every curtain shut, stacked furniture against every window and door, stripped all the bedding, pulled all her clothes from her hangars, and slammed them into the washing machine, hoping to get rid of every single last particle of him. She pulled her mattress from the bed, and used it to block the bathroom door off, hoping that if X decided to break in again through the broken window, the temporary barrier would give her enough time to escape out the front door.

As the bundled clothes and sheets spun around in the washer, she found a hand held-mirror, and carefully stuffed a tampon up each nostril, watching, aghast, as two black eyes bloomed in her swollen face.

And then, another letter came. It slid under

her front door like a snake, and Laura watched it, whimpering.

Dear Laura,

Now you know that I'm not lying, don't you? I'm sorry about your face. I couldn't let you take my photo to the Police. I thought we were building trust, Laura. Now it feels like we've gone back a step.

I was upset by your letter, Laura. The one you wrote when you moved out. Did you think I wouldn't follow you? That is not how this works. You don't get to write the letters, because I'm the one that has what you want. You don't get to tell me what to do. Only I get to make the rules.

I've decided to forgive you for not trusting me, but in exchange for the next clue, and as a way of proving to me how sorry you are, I need something special.

Laura felt as if the power balance had tilted in his favour once again. He held the keys to her future, her happiness, and her peace of mind, and he knew it, fed off of her helplessness. Any attempt she made to go to the Police now could end in her death. And a photograph of her own, filled with red.

She continued reading, a cold sheen of sweat collecting on her brow.

A tooth, said the letter. *A big tooth, a molar. Give me what I want, and I'll give you a clue.*

Deep down inside, you know you can't live without me, don't you? And I can't live without you for much longer, Laura. If you don't do as I say, I'm not sure I can hold myself back.

No cheating. I'll know if it's not your tooth.
Yours with respect,
X

Laura dropped the letter and watched as it glided to the floor.

And she realised something, as his words stared up at her from her feet.

This was no longer about Bobby. Maybe it never really had been.

This was about her, and him.

This was his obsession, coming to a climax. All he had ever wanted to do was own pieces of her, and hurt the rest. Bobby was long dead, and she was the target, but if she tried to go back to the Police, he would kill her. She remembered the size of him, the weight of his fist.

And he knew where she lived.

Her mind raced with a thousand different scenarios, all of them ending the same way: with X, pinning her down, reaching into her wide open mouth with a chisel, or some pliers, or maybe even a knife. X, using a felt-tip pen to draw a thin line around her neck, just above the clavicle. X, working on her body with a sharp tool, like an electric saw, or kitchen knife.

He had killed Bobby this way, and he would kill her unless she did as she was told.

Was there really no other way?

Even if she left the house today, somehow, without him noticing, which seemed impossible...

she had nowhere to go. She couldn't afford a hotel, and he knew where her parents lived. Her boyfriend would take her in, but she didn't want to put him in any danger, because that's what this was, now: life, or death.

She thought about it until her brain ached, and then, came to a single, devastating conclusion.

What was her life worth, really, when she thought about it?

A full set of teeth?

Maybe, after this, he would stop.

Maybe, after this, it would be enough.

It's only a tooth, Laura, she told herself. *Only a tooth.*

She went to fetch a hammer and a pair of pliers from the toolbox she kept under her sink. She downed a cheap bottle of wine. Took a hold of her right back molar with the pliers.

Pulled, hard.

The tooth didn't budge.

It's only a tooth, goddamn it! How hard can it be?

She tried again, swollen eyes spilling over from effort and from pain, but an innate and instinctive desire to protect her body from wilful mutilation kicked in, and she had to stop. Laura realised she was not going to be able to pull the tooth out without some creativity.

Haunted by the image of her darling Bobby with his arms wrapped around a mystery man, she searched for, and found, more alcohol, and a small wrap of cannabis that her boyfriend had hidden on top of a kitchen cabinet. She rolled a large, messy spliff, and fantasized about what she would do, when she was free of it all. A house by the sea, perhaps. A dog. Maybe even a child, one day. The possibilities were limitless, if she could only break free of this terrible bondage, this terrible pact she had somehow entered into. Command, and obey. Suffer, in silence. An eye for an eye.

A tooth for a tooth.

She picked up the pliers again.

And this time, she didn't stop.

19.

Her boyfriend found her lying on the floor of her kitchenette, blood everywhere, a single, broken molar lying in the palm of her hand. He stared, speechless, as she lay in her own mess, conscious, but unmoving. Her nose was swollen and lopsided, her eyes were two large black shadows in her face, and her mouth dribbled congealed blood and splinters of tooth. In a panic, he called an ambulance, which took her to the hospital, where he stayed with her as they reset her nose and patched up her mouth. He was angry, confused, and aware suddenly that Laura had secrets beyond his comprehension.

Unbeknownst to him, a tall man in a dark blue t-shirt ambled up and down the car-park outside the accident and emergency ward, pulling a now very old black and white collie dog behind him. He did this for hours, until Laura was discharged, and watched as she left in a taxi with her boyfriend.

Then, he left, and the collie left with him.

Laura broke her relationship off four days

later. A parting of ways had been brewing for a while, anyway, largely due to her own fear of intimacy. And she realised that she just couldn't bear to let anyone else into the sad, desperate triangle that was Bobby, X and her. Her ex seemed relieved: she'd thought he might, after their trip to the hospital. Who would want to date a woman who pulled out her own, perfectly healthy, teeth? He wished her well, politely, and she did the same, and that was that. She was alone again.

Apart from X.

The tooth she wrapped in cling film, and left in a small alcove in the wall near her apartment's front door. One hour later, the tooth was gone, and she allowed herself to tentatively hope for a small respite, as X enjoyed the fruits of her labour.

Eventually, she went back to work, as if nothing at all of consequence had happened, her face bruised, her cheek swollen, her nose patched up with surgical strips.

And nobody much questioned her about it, because they knew she wouldn't tell them anyway. She was mystery wrapped in silence, and sometimes, unwrapping the secret just wasn't worth the struggle.

20.

By six in the morning, the forest was fully awake. Laura saw ponies in a clearing, cropping a patchy carpet of grass with strong, blunt teeth, tails swishing as they flicked insects away from their sensitive hides. She wished she had time to stop and appreciate the beauty of the moment. But she didn't. She was on a tight schedule. Her proximity to her goal gave her renewed strength, and adrenaline helped her where resolve petered out. She did pause, later, just long enough to apply a fresh wound dressing to her swollen ankle. She recognised the early signs of infection, recognised them and ignored them, swallowing more paracetamol. As she returned her first aid kit to her pack, her hand brushed against the bundle at the bottom of the bag, the heavy item wrapped in a towel. She hesitated, and wondered if now was the time to unwrap it, tuck it into the waistband of her trousers, as she'd seen people do in the movies. She decided against it. It would get in the way, there, be a nuisance as she walked. The gun stayed where it was. She felt it pressing into the small of her back with every step.

As she walked, she tongued the empty spot on her gum where her back molar had once grown.

21.

After the tooth, Laura's world descended into darkness, paranoia, and extreme caution. Her gum turned sceptic, and despite her best efforts to stay away, eventually she had to take numerous trips, via taxi, to the dentist. Trips that she couldn't afford, to remove bits of the molar's root that had been left behind by her clumsy extraction, causing the infection.

She carried on working, but her habits changed. She switched to day-shifts, so that more staff were on site, and even then, often called in sick, feeling too afraid to leave the house. When she did manage it, she learned to run, fast, to the bus stop. She took the bus into town, rather than walking, so that she was always surrounded by people. She never sat on the top deck alone, either, sitting down below, as close to the driver as possible.

In between visits to the dentist chair and shifts at the supermarket she waited for the clues she was owed, but nothing happened. She found this impossible to bear, particularly after the photographs. She tried not to think about what X did with the things she sent him. What had he done with her tooth? Put it on a thong around his neck? Placed it in a trinket box? Slotted it into his own mouth, pretended to be her? Thrown it away? Somehow, the last option was the worst of all, because it implied that her sacrifice was unimportant, that the only thing that mattered was controlling her.

Her anxiety increased steadily until she began to experience crippling physical symptoms: panic attacks, vast, insurmountable waves of dread that crashed into her at the most unexpected of moments and rendered her incoherent, unable to breathe, or move, or do anything except sit, frozen in paralysis, until it passed. She was lucky that her job was not a customer-facing role. When the attacks happened to her during a shift, she was largely unobserved, as other night-shifters were few in numbers. She simply stood there, packaged food in hand, rigid, hyperventilating, shaking, mouth hanging open uselessly, until it passed. At home, she developed a reliance on cannabis to help her manage. She took out a loan, and then another, to finance her habit and her dental work.

She moved, planning the operation with military levels of precision so that she left, via taxi, in the middle of the night. She insisted that the taxi driver met her at her door, and escorted her to the next. Leaving the majority of her possessions behind, she took only what she could fit into a large, canvas holdall, and relocated under the cover of the dark. Her new place was a top floor apartment where the windows were too high to climb into, and she made sure that her door had a peep-hole, too.

Laura grew thin, diminished, consumed by her neuroses.

Then, somehow, her birthday arrived. Another one, another day she simultaneously feared and hated, now, for so many reasons. It came, and passed, and not only was there no letter, but she had little in the way of anything, as her mother had been taken ill and wasn't able to post her card until days later. She sifted through the mail on her doormat and found only bills, junk mail, and a flyer from the local MP, trying to garner votes.

Was she being punished still, she wondered, for going to the Police, or was he just torturing her, because that was how he operated?

She stared at the letterbox for hours, almost hoping to see a large, looming shadow behind the door, but the shadow never came. She pressed her eye to the peephole, looking for the distorted, fish-lens version of him in the hallway, but it remained empty. And no letter came. Not that day, or the next, or the next. Had she done it? Had she really done it, this time? Had she slipped the net?

Time went by, during which it began to dawn on Laura that something might have happened to X. There had been silences before, but this was different. They had unfinished business. He owed her for the tooth, and so far, he'd always paid his dues. He had a strange and warped code of honour like that.

Laura began to tentatively speculate as to

what had happened to her pen pal. He'd moved away, or was in prison, or even- and this hurt her more than she could bring herself to understand- maybe, even, he had died.

Imagine that. Imagine if X were dead.

She couldn't.

On the one hand, she would be free of him.

But on the other, she never would, not as long as she remembered that photo of Bobby. The one painted in red.

X's silence dragged on, and the nature of it almost broke her. Almost. She spiralled into a hole of work and weed, work and weed, and fretful, broken sleep. She began to lose grip on all sense of what was real, and what wasn't. Bobby came to her in dreams, his hair long, and matted with blood, and his face was always a blank featureless smudge that shimmered and jittered the longer she looked at it. Her memories were being eaten away, one by one, and it was only through old photographs and notes that they had written to each other at school that she could recall much about him at all. Such childish notes, they were, too, riddled with scribbles and doodles and superlatives. Notes about stupid things like television shows and music and who was on which sports team, notes which held no hint of the things to come for either of them. They made her sad and furious at the same time, and she longed for a time when her mood and her health were not governed by the words scrawled onto a piece of paper, childish or otherwise.

Eventually, Laura's workplace forced her to take some sick leave, reluctant to let her go because she was a good worker, but unable to deal with her increasingly bizarre and unpredictable behaviour. With so much time on her hands, she crashed further down into despair, getting high and revisiting each and every location from the letters that she had coordinates for, ritually, one by one, in her mind. Even the spot located in the supermarket frozen food aisle. But when she got there, she found that the passage of time had not changed anything about her predicament at all. Bobby was still not there. Bobby was not anywhere. Bobby was dead, his body in pieces. Once again, she thought about burning the letters. Once again, she thought about going to the Police. She did neither. Instead, she longed for release.

One day bled into the next, and the next, and so on, with no word from X, until she looked in the mirror and saw a single grey hair. Years had passed. Five more. She was still living in the same tiny studio flat, still had the same minimum-wage job.

And she still had no new letters.

Instead of being happy about it, she was wretched, held captive by something so complicated she didn't know how to give it a name.

And then, one day, whilst hoisting a pack of rice up onto a high shelf at work, she met Frank.

And everything changed.

22.

Frank was unlike anyone she'd ever met before. The first thing that struck her was how much he resembled Bobby. Or how much she *thought* he resembled Bobby given her patchy memory.

He was tall, unusually so, and had blonde, straight hair that fell in a curtain across his face. When she first saw him, she nearly fell off of the step-ladder she was perched on top of. When she first saw him, she thought that Bobby had come back for her, after all this time. For a fleeting moment she held onto the hope, and then she remembered the photo. Frank drew closer. He smiled up at her, and Laura could see that it wasn't Bobby. But the resemblance was strong enough to trigger a massive response.

He asked her a question. Laura saw his mouth moving, but couldn't hear the words he was saying. A cold rush of adrenaline had rocketed through her veins, and she fought desperately against a panic attack. Fought, and lost. Her nostrils flared, the blood pounded in her ears, and her mouth dropped open as she fought for breath.

Frank did something very unexpected, then. He stood on tiptoes, reached up and took the bag of rice from her hands, and dropped it on the floor. It split, rice spurting out everywhere, but he ignored it. Instead, he joined her on the stepladder, so that she stood higher than him, but they were still close enough to touch. He reached out and placed a hand carefully on her shoulder. She reared back, almost toppling from the ladder, and he removed his hand, then tried again. This time, she let him touch her.

'If you can,' he said, 'Try to breathe out more than you breathe in. It'll help. I can show you, if you'd like?'

She couldn't reply. She just stared at him, her eyes wide. Who was this person? What was he talking about? Could it be possible...did he understand, somehow, what was happening to her?

He didn't wait for confirmation. Instead, he took a great, deep breath, and blew it out gently through his cheeks, a long exhale, longer than the inhale. He repeated the movement, and then did it a third time, and Laura realised distantly that he was counting in his head. He breathed out for double the amount of time he breathed in. He was counting it, in his head, just for her, so that she could learn.

In, one, two, three.

Out, one, two, three, four, five, and six.

In, one, two, three.

It was almost like dancing, except the only music was her distress.

Gradually, her own chest began to rise

and fall in sync with his. They kept eye-contact throughout the entire exchange. His was steady, and kind. Hers was frightened, yet compelled.

She read somewhere once, in one of those magazines friends used to buy her, in that brief period when she'd had friends, that it took only a few minutes of steady eye-contact to fall in love.

Steady eye-contact, and steady breathing, and one bag of spilled rice.

They stayed like that for a long time, and all thoughts of Bobby, and X, vanished from her mind in that small, blissful window where Frank took control, and cared for her.

He explained it to her, later, when they were naked in his bed. She was too afraid to take him to her place, but Frank had a car, and she figured that if X was watching her, he would find it more difficult to track her if she was in a stranger's vehicle, moving at speed. So, she took a risk, the first one she'd taken in years, and the risk felt, at last, like it was worth it.

'It's to do with oxygen and carbon dioxide levels in your body,' Frank said, stroking the soft skin around her nipples. They hardened in response. 'When you freak out, you breathe in too much, take too much oxygen in. You need carbon dioxide in your brain too.'

Laura said nothing, just lay in the crook of his arm, letting his fingers move down, tracing the line from navel to groin, and marvelling at how unafraid she felt lying next to him.

'You're probably wondering how I know all this,' he continued, but she didn't take the bait. She didn't want to know, in that moment. All she wanted was to lie there and enjoy something, for once. His fingers moved inside of her, and Laura, mesmerised by the sensation, felt like she were slowly waking up from a terrible nightmare. Which was exactly what she *was* doing.

Later, it transpired that Frank had been in a car accident, as a child. He'd struggled with anxiety ever since. Laura took this information, and thought about swapping it for her own story, the story of Bobby, and the letters, and X, and the codes, and her missing back molar. But she didn't.

Even when they married, she didn't.

Even when, red-faced and roaring, she pushed out her beautiful baby boy, and called him Robert, and marvelled at his white-blonde hair. Still, she said nothing.

She kept her secrets, and time flew past like water tumbling across a great fall, and her family took root, flourished, blossomed, and she smiled again.

And no letters came.

As she thrived, conversely, others did not, as if the scales of life found themselves unbalanced, and compensated accordingly. Mr and Mrs. Eveleigh divorced, grew older and developed health problems, and eventually, Bobby's mother died, having never found out what happened to her boy. The newspapers loved the tragedy inherent in her not knowing, and, circling around her more insistently as she deteriorated, pestered her for interviews. She gave one, eventually, to a national tabloid six months before she passed. It was the usual fare: a harrowing plea for information that felt, because it was, like a drowning woman clutching at air. *'The worst thing,'* the article concluded, *'is not knowing what happened to Bobby. It's the not knowing.'*

Laura, the keeper of secrets, wondered how true this actually was. She suspected that knowledge would be just as dreadful for Bobby's parents to cope with as the lack of closure. She suspected that *not* knowing had saved them some considerable distress. Who was to say? Mrs. Eveleigh had dwelt in anger for such a long time. It was unlikely any news in either direction would have revived her lost equilibrium. Her picture haunted Laura for a whole day as it stared out of the folded newspaper on the breakfast table. Mrs. Eveleigh's eyes, rendered dark and flat by the poor print quality of the paper, followed her around the room, and, it felt, beyond. *Why didn't you do more?* They said, accusingly. *Why didn't you tell us what you knew?*

Laura didn't go to Mrs. Eveleigh's funeral, not out of anger, or spite, but out of a desire not to upset the family any more than they already had been. Seeing Laura might remind the Eveleighs of just how much they had lost. The chance to watch him wed, the chance to hold a grandchild. And the memories of Bobby's service still clung to her. Candles, and prayers, and meaningless, insincere words floating up into the vaulted ceiling spaces.

And Tara Eveleigh's eyes, staring her out of the church.

Laura kept her secrets. Time passed over her, and she folded all the parts of herself that related to Bobby and X and the letters into a neat, compact package, and mentally filed it away. She finally allowed herself, as she approached middle age, to admit that X was gone. He had finished with her. Maybe the tooth had been enough, after all. Maybe he had found a new obsession. Maybe he had died. This thought no longer scared her like it used to. She was a parent now, and X was a threat to her family, a threat she couldn't afford. She had her own path, her own responsibilities, her own Bobby. She had purpose, and identity. X belonged in the past, along with her youth.

And then, when she was forty-four, on the morning of her birthday, it happened.

She got another envelope.

Laura, it said on the front of the dingy yellow packet. The word was written in a familiar hand, shakier, but instantly recognisable.

The world fell away from her. Or was it she who was falling? Endlessly, through a dark space, the ground continually threatening to surge up from beneath and smash her to pieces, only it never seemed to get there, somehow. She just kept falling.

Inside the envelope were two things. A letter, with a string of coordinates. This was par for the course, with X.

And a cloth badge, which was not. On it was embroidered a school insignia. The thread was worn and furry, the colours bleached, but she knew instantly what it was. It was her old school insignia. There was a shield, with a tree growing behind, and two rabbits entwined around the base. The badge had been cut from a dark green woollen sweater. The same type of sweater that both she and Bobby had been wearing on the day he climbed into the van.

The badge was also spattered with a dark, rusty brown substance that she knew, without question, was blood.

Bobby's blood.

Laura saw this, and still could not cry.

Instead, she just kept falling.

23.

Dear Laura

By now, you are forty-four years old. I remember that age. I was near that age when I first met Bobby, and first saw you. Now I am an old man, and time has not been good to me.

I am sorry I didn't write before. I was put away for something I did. Locked up like an animal, by people who don't understand what real feelings are. People don't know love, not the way I do. Society judges me instead. I couldn't write from prison. I couldn't risk them finding out about Bobby. He is our secret, isn't he? So I stopped writing, for his sake. It was agony for me. But I thought about you every day, Laura. Every single day.

They let me out on good behaviour in the end, although sometimes I wish they had kept me inside, where I had a bed and hot food. I don't have those things now. My health is not so good. Time is running out for me. Will you mourn for me when I'm finally gone? I hope so, Laura. I mourn for Bobby.

We still never finished with Bobby, did we? That's why I am sending his school badge. I am sorry there is so much blood on it. I tried to clean him up but it was difficult, and I got frustrated. I am worried you have forgotten about him, and me. I have missed you. I feel like maybe I love you, although it is such a shame you had to grow up so much.

I am sad that you got married Laura. I thought our connection was the special one. But now you have someone else. I'm not sure I can allow it.

Perhaps if you come and see me we can talk about it. I'm old, as I said. I feel that it's finally time. I would like to meet at the place I buried Bobby. Alone. No Police- you know the rule.

Join the dots, and come soon. Come by seven-thirty in the morning, in three days' time. If you don't, I will come after your boy, and I will take him like I took Bobby. And then, I think it quite likely that I shall die. I'm sick, you see.

Don't be angry with me, Laura. I feel good knowing that despite losing Bobby, I have been able to write to you, and you know I exist. That must mean something to you too. I think ours was always the real love story, Laura. Not me and Bobby.

Yours with respect (and love)
X

After the X, a list of digits and symbols marched down the paper, a bewildering string of them, and once again, as they had when she was young, they danced, and leapt across her vision.

Coordinates.

24.

'**Laura?** What is it?' Said Frank, looking at her over his newspaper as she sat there dumbly holding the letter, falling, falling, the only way being down.

At first, she didn't reply, but then, she took a deep breath. 'Nothing,' she lied, brightly, folding the letter and putting it into her shirt pocket. Because once a secret has grown old, and burrowed itself like a tick under the skin, it is harder to dig out than she could fathom. Frank side-eyed her, but didn't push the matter. It was her birthday, and he wanted her to have a nice day. Frank was like that. He put others before himself as a matter of principle. Doing so gave him a great and lasting satisfaction. She had thought several times that Frank would have made a good priest, or vicar. She felt now, after years of marriage, as she had felt then, when she'd first met him: that Frank was on a mission. He used the accident he'd had as a child as a springboard, diving into a pool of vocation, striking out confidently across the choppy waters towards anyone he found drowning. Frank was the sort of person who would die to keep you afloat. She had tried to do the same, over the years, for others, only it was a much less convincing display than Frank's. But she tried.

Later, when Frank went out to run some errands, she read the letter again.

Join the dots, X had said, and she analysed and re-analysed this several times before it clicked, and then she smacked her hand to her forehead hard in an act of realisation.

Of course!

She dug around under her comfortable king-sized bed for the storage box she kept there, full of memories, clippings and correspondence. The letters from X were buried at the bottom of the box, along with her old map and compass. She had kept it all. Maybe because, deep down, her subconscious mind had known this day was coming, after all.

She spread the map out across her bed, and unfolded each letter she'd ever received from X, reminding herself of the contents, shaking her head and muttering to herself the whole time. She'd never taken a step back from it, like this, and looked at the letters all together, as a complete entity. She'd only ever treated each one as an individual step towards downfall, but now...now, here on her bed, was a finished jigsaw puzzle. A portrait of a man. What kind of man? A criminal, she knew that now. A repeat offender? Most likely a paedophile, too, which is something she had never openly admitted to herself until now. *What a shame you had to grow up,* he'd said. She shuddered as she remembered wrapping up a pair of her knickers for him. And the tooth. The hammer. The blood. What *had* he done with it all? Did he have a memory box too, full of all the pieces of her she'd sent him?

She realised, as she looked at it all laid out across her patchwork bedspread, that over the years, all she'd done was exacerbate his obsession with her by alternately rejecting him, trying to run from him, and then giving in to his demands. She realised now, with the advent of maturity and the wisdom that parenthood had afforded her, that X had manipulated her from a young age. He had preyed upon her guilt and confusion, and twisted her fear around his strange declarations of love for herself, and for Bobby. And Laura had bought into this fantasy narrative, bought a map, gone on bus journeys, smashed a hammer into her own mouth and pulled a tooth for him, even written back. All grist for his sordid mill. Laura had been the object of X's desire for all these years, not Bobby. Laura.

Laura.

And here he was again, still trying to write their story.

Still no tears. Laura shook all over, and still no tears. *Why can't I cry?* She thought with desperation.

Why?

Had there been others? She thought it likely. X was obsessive by nature. His letters also had a curious air of being practised about them, like maybe he had honed his skills on someone before her. Had he sent letters to Bobby in the years before he disappeared? She thought that likely too, although no mention of it had ever been made by the Eveleighs.

The Police. This all needed to go to the Police. X was an old man, now. He would not be waiting to knock her down this time if she strode into town with a handbag full of evidence. She should take this letter, and all the others, to the Police, and tell them what she knew. They would not dismiss her now. She was a respectable age, a Mother, a well-liked person in the community. She came with added gravitas.

And yet...

And yet.

She *was* in her forties, a mother, a wife, an administrator of a local victim support charity alongside Frank, an advocate for mental health and a child safety awareness campaigner. All of the pain and loss and confusion had been scooped up, and poured into better, worthier pastimes than trying to piece together the demented clues that X had left, uninvited, on her doormat as a young girl.

Laura was beyond all of that, now, wasn't she? This was a matter, at last, for the authorities. X was old, now, and sick, he said it himself. What reprisals would there be, if she handed everything in?

And yet.

I will come after your boy, and I will take him like I took Bobby.

The threat dangled in the air before her, and

try as she might, she couldn't ignore it. The dissonant chords of long repressed memory jangled in her mind, and scenes flashed in front of her eyes: a van, idling on the curb. A boy, blonde hair hanging in soft curtains around his face, climbing in through the open door. A shadow, lurking behind the frosted glass of her parent's front door. A fist, slamming into her face. A tooth, lying in a puddle of gore in the palm of her hand. Envelopes, on the doormat. A photo, filled with red. He might be old, but he was practised. Motivated. And he'd been in prison, so he might know people. People who could help him hurt her, help him take her little boy.

He was dangerous.

And she believed him. She believed he could do it. He had done it before, and he wanted to do it again.

How could she ignore that? Worse, trust the Police with this information?

And besides all of this, despite coming to terms with not wanting to know Bobby's fate, the question of where his remains had been all these years still gaped open, like a wound. Imagine if she could find him, after all. Imagine if she could bring him back to his family for a proper goodbye.

Because the knife still twisted, in rare quiet moments where she found herself without a task. All these years later, it twisted, and she felt the ghost of Bobby's hand upon hers. Her lips tingled beneath his kiss, breathy and hesitant. So young. They had both been so young.

Laura looked at her worn, dog-eared map. She saw deliberate red splotches across contour-lines: the coordinates from all the other letters, marks that she had made in permanent ink. Her fingers twitched with the memory of scribbling forcefully on that detailed and intricate surface. Carefully, her heart climbing slowly back up into her throat like it used to when she was younger, she studied his last letter, and the list of numbers he'd provided at the end. Then, with a marker pen she found on Frank's writing desk, she tentatively marked the final coordinates on the map.

And the last, vital piece fell into place.

Join the dots, he'd said. With trembling hands, she did as she was told, because she always did what X told her to. She began to connect the dots, and gradually, his design became apparent.

She saw concentric rings form beneath her hands, not circles exactly, but rings like those of a tree, closing in around a single point, a small area in the vast expanse of the Old Forest, the size of the tip of her thumb against the map.

In the middle of this space, a clearing was marked, with a thin stream bisecting it. The area was no more than twenty feet wide, she guessed, from the scale on the map, although distance was hard to accurately judge by her eye alone.

Somewhere, in that area, she would find the man who wrote the letters.

Somewhere, in that area, she knew she would also find Bobby.

She made one final, damning mark on the map with jerky, uncooperative fingers. And when she saw what she'd written, she laughed, out loud, because all she could do now was resort to humour, every other emotion in her repertoire having long since been used. 'X', it said.

X marks the spot.

25.

The trees sang to her as she walked. Tiny, whispering songs that skittered past her ears and rose and fell with the thin morning breeze. A rabbit froze in the path ahead of her, head rigid, eyes dark and wide, and then it ran, white tail flashing as it bounded away into the undergrowth. Somewhere, a jay called out, harsh, mocking. The compass and the map thump, thump, thumped against her chest. Her hair no longer fell into her eyes, but frizzed out into a cloud around her head, humidity, grease and a night's rough sleep taking its toll.

She walked, and with every step she took, she felt taller, and colder, and more rigid, as if she were one of the very trees themselves, uprooted, marching to war.

And then, she found it. The place she'd been searching for. Thirty years of her life, spent looking.

She knew it as soon as she saw it: this, after all, was the land in her heart, the Promised Land, the place she had been flying towards, even when she had thought she was not. It had lived inside her for so long that she was afraid she wouldn't recognise it when she arrived, but here she was, at seven in the morning, earlier than requested, bloodied, bruised, and cold. A little brown bird, exhausted, migrating north to that one, fixed target.

She had come, suddenly, to the clearing in the forest, stumbled upon it before sensing a change in the density of the trees and light overhead. Passing from shade to bright, she looked up and saw a window of pale blue sky. High up there, way up in the air, a tiny white plane flew, arrow-straight, trails of white chasing behind. Laura took a deep breath, and stepped further into the clearing.

It was filled with clutter and camping equipment and bags of stinking, rotting rubbish. Sunlight dappled the top of an old blue tarpaulin, mildewed from being long exposed to the elements. It was stretched out from one tree to another by ropes, to form a makeshift roof. Underneath this, there stood a sagging fortress of bedding. Mattresses piled up against each other to form doughy walls, bed springs erupting from their stuffing in mad, vicious coils. A random assortment of carpet scraps were littered across the ground, and a few sheets of rusty corrugated iron leaned haphazardly against nearby tree trunks to act as weatherproofing. A tattered groundsheet, rubber tyres, and large, wind-felled branches completed the structure.

This was it, she knew it. She knew it in her bones. This was where X was living, maybe this is where he had been living all of his life, when not in prison. The shelter was not a new structure. Mature saplings thrust themselves up between gaps in the tarpaulin, and brambles and ferns entangled themselves protectively around the entire mess in a well-established, thorny embrace. Discarded propane cylinders lay all around, years' worth, and a makeshift laundry line hung across one side of the clearing, over which a worn pair of boxer shorts, some black, threadbare socks and a sheet of torn plastic were hung. They steamed faintly as the morning sun gathered in strength and burned away the night-time dew.

She imagined him, hunched over, meaty fists wrapped around a cheap pen, writing letters to her from his mattress cocoon and folding them into dirty yellow envelopes while the trees shook their leaves overhead in judgement.

This was his home, his turf, his front door.

And this was where she would find Bobby.

She gently lowered her backpack to the ground, seeing no sign of anyone who could be X. The place was eerily peaceful, but if she had her way, that peace wouldn't last.

She slid a hand inside her pack, and brought out the towel-wrapped gun. It was Frank's gun, a family heirloom that had belonged to his Grandfather. She knew little about such things, but she did know it had seen some action in the Second World War. It wasn't loaded, according to Frank, and she wasn't even sure it worked properly anymore, but it was enough. Enough to threaten a man, and drive her point home. All Laura wanted to do was scare X the way he had scared her. All she wanted to do was see fear in his eyes, and fight back, let him see he no longer controlled her. Scare him away from her life and her family. She didn't want to hurt him, because it wasn't in her to harm another, and besides- that would make her no better than he was. But she *was* owed fear. And much, much more besides.

Quid pro quo, you suffer, I suffer, she thought, and slid the gun into a pocket, eyes constantly scanning the clearing, looking for X. Where was he? Was he hiding? Then, she changed her mind, and took the weapon out again, deciding she would hold it loosely by her side, a more obvious deterrent there, the solid weight of it comforting in her hand.

Suddenly, she heard coughing. Heavy, phlegm-stuffed coughing, coming from a discarded sofa she'd not noticed until that point. He eyes whipped across the clearing and took a few seconds to make it out, but there it sat, rotting and almost completely camouflaged by nettles- a large, lop-sided, brown faux-leather couch, outer layer of skin peeling off in large strips as if flayed, bright green mildew filling in the patches exposed beneath.

And there, reclining on the torn and slimy upholstery, belly out, arms behind his head, watching, waiting, there, after all these years, was her pen pal.

X.

26.

Laura moved slowly across the clearing, gun cold and heavy and awkward in her unpractised hand. She approached the sofa, upon which lay the bulbous form of X, and tasted sour bile in her mouth. Here he was, the man who had taken Bobby away. Here he was, the man who wanted her used knickers and sanitary towels. Here he was, the man who had made her pull her own tooth out.

Reposed, he looked bucolic, almost, like a fallen tree trunk, a part of the forest. He was dressed in a camouflaged, military style jacket splattered with patches of brown, green and grey. Underneath, he wore a dark blue t-shirt that was too small for him. It rode up above his stomach, which was pale, and hairy, the belly button lost in a soft crease of fat. Laura felt like she recognised the blue shirt from the day he had attacked her, but she couldn't be sure. Underneath, he had squeezed into poorly fitting camouflage trousers, and under those sat two dirty, worn Nike trainers with the soles flapping freely from both feet.

She studied him with a distant curiosity as

she approached. He had a beard, and a bulbous nose, and she was reminded, absurdly, of pictures and carvings she'd seen of the Green Man, deity of the forest. He was dirty, and smelled of urine and mud and sweat, even from several feet away. Mosquitos gathered around his exposed hands and ankles, but he seemed unconcerned by them, letting them land, bite and drink without slapping a single one away.

Laura took a step closer, then another, then another, the dull throb in her ankle a constant reminder of how far she'd come to be here. She held the gun out before her, rigid, in a warning gesture. His deep-set eyes glittered in his face. She came to a stop before him, just out of arm's reach.

'I'm here,' she said, at last, her voice weak and unsteady, and X laughed, lazily craning his neck and checking an ancient wind-up watch on his filthy wrist.

'You're early,' he wheezed, and Laura wished, suddenly, with all her heart, that the gun was loaded.

27.

'**I've** waited a long time to meet you, Laura.'

The gun wobbled in her hand, and her arm ached from the effort of holding it out and keeping it pointed at his head.

'I don't care,' she said, not willing to engage with anything except the reason she had come: to tell him to leave her alone.

X watched her, and she watched X. Overhead, the plane disappeared from view, its twin streams breaking up into foamy clouds, then dissipating. The quiet thickened. It seemed, after being so talkative in his letters, that X was not as forthcoming in person, content to let the silence between them stretch out further and further. Laura knew this instinctively to be a power play, knew that whoever broke the standoff first would lose somehow, but she was beyond caring, beyond playing games.

'Where is he?' She asked, blood ringing in her ears. 'Where is Bobby?'

X propped himself up slowly on one arm, and then painfully, awkwardly heaved himself upright on the couch.

'Do you want to see my scars?' He said, lifting his shirt up and showing off his pigeon chest. His gut protruded out from beneath it like a swollen, ridiculous tumour. She saw pale, shiny marks criss-crossing the skin between his nipples, and then she realised the scars were arranged in the form of let-ters, a crude inscription that someone had carved onto his body: PAEDO, it read.

'They don't like people like me in prison,' he said, by way of explanation, and then coughed, his belly wobbling and convulsing as he hacked and spat. Laura had never been so repulsed by anything in her life.

'Where is Bobby?' She repeated, and X lapsed back into silence, breathing hard through his mouth, his face and eyes red, and raw. Laura's nerve was failing. The impetus she'd felt when she'd re-ceived his final letter had petered out, and now that the journey was complete, the constant act of mov-ing forward no longer the thing keeping her sane, the fear and doubt surrounding her bizarre situ-ation began crashing in, like water through a burst dam.

'Your hair is going grey,' he said, at last, and Laura couldn't contain it anymore. He didn't know where Bobby was, he never had. He was still playing the game, and the game wouldn't be done until she was broken, because that was what he had decided to make his life about. There was no Bobby, there was no end, only him, and her, until he died, and let her be, and even then she would dream of this moment, she knew it. She would wake in the night, breath stuck tight in her throat, and see only one thing: X, reclining in his throne, scrutinising her, criticising her temerity for letting herself age.

And she realised, in that moment, how angry X was with her for not being a thirteen-year-old girl anymore. How angry he had always been.

Having never once cried in her entire adult life, the tears that had solidified like resin about her heart suddenly liquefied, and ran free, and Laura burst into tears, gun wobbling about as her whole body shook with the force of her distress.

And X sat, on his couch, hands resting loosely by his sides, and watched, a small, triumphant smile upon his lips.

Then, he reached into the collar of his shirt, and brought something out. Something small, and white, the colour of bone.

Her tooth.

The tears kept coming, and she feared they might never stop. She cried so hard she nearly vomited, mouth open, retching with the force, eyes swelling and tight, face wet in the morning sun.

She'd been right. He wore her tooth on a thin wire necklace around his neck. It swung back and forth, and she gazed at it, aghast, remembering the day she'd taken a hammer to herself. The tears kept coming, and then something else made its presence known. A pressurised feeling, as if a great bubble of air were rising up from somewhere deep inside.

'Thank you for this,' X croaked, enjoying her

anguish, his voice suffused with a horrible intensity.

And the bubble shot into her mouth and burst out of her, only it wasn't a bubble, it wasn't air, it was a scream, a scream that had been brewing for thirty odd years, and it propelled her forward as it ricocheted around the clearing, and the gun might not have been loaded, but it was heavy, and solid, and she brought it down on X's face, as hard as she could, and kept bringing it down, until he was no longer smiling, until his own rotten teeth had smashed and splintered, until she felt his nose crunch under the butt of the gun, and all she could think was *quid pro quo*, over and over, until she was spent.

28.

Afterwards, she sat on the forest floor, and gathered herself, as best she could. The gun she kept a tight hold of, slick as it was with blood and gore. She looked at X, and looked at the damage she'd wrought. She could see the light flutter of his chest, labouring for air. X was alive, but unconscious, and for that, she was intensely, unspeakably grateful. If he was alive, then she wasn't a murderer. If he was alive, then she had a chance at a future, and her son would still have a Mother.

She realised the wetness on her face was no longer from her own tears, and ran the back of her hand down one cheek. It came away red, and slippery, and a little swell of cold, irrational victory bloomed.

She should leave, now, she knew, leave X here in the woods to live his life in filth, to drink cold tinned soup through a broken mouth and snore through a broken nose. She had taught him a lesson, given back some of the pain he'd gifted her. She wasn't proud of it…or was she? Either way, it was done. So, she should leave.

But she didn't. Something held her back.

One, final hesitancy.

Bobby.

And then, as if nature itself had decided to make a friend of her rather than an enemy, she heard something fall from a tree behind her, and land on the ground with a hard and distinct thump.

Her head whipped around, and the gun came up, but there was nothing there except for a squirrel, who had dropped a nut from his place high up in the canopy and was now scooting back down the thick oak trunk to retrieve it.

And something else, sticking out amongst the roots of the tree, lopsided, crude, and weathered.

A wooden cross.

Upon it, a name, painted in faded blue.

Bobby.

29.

There was bone, barely concealed under a thin layer of soil. It was a shallower grave than she had imagined it would be. It stuck out from the broken ground, white against dark, jagged, broken edges pointing skyward. Laura kept digging with the trowel she had packed especially for this purpose, not content with one, single bone. *I need all of you*, she thought. *Every single piece. I want it all back. All of it. Each part of you.*

The animals of the woodland watched her from afar as she dug, frantic arcs of flung earth spraying all around her, her breath coming thick and fast, her eyes bright with exertion, darkening blood still splattered across her face. They watched and listened to the desperate, urgent sounds that fell from her lips as she dug. Every now and then, she would stop, and extract bone, and lay it on a tarpaulin spread out next to her.

She felt like an archaeologist, felt as if she should be labelling each fragment and splinter, so that Bobby could be reassembled, later, like a jigsaw, and, in doing so, she could finally hold him, and say what she never had a chance to say when she was thirteen. *Goodbye.* It was all she had wanted. That one word. A chance to say it.

The trowel cut through the dank earth and brought up lumps of root, and stone, and moss, and bone, so much bone, and she marvelled at how many bones there were in a fifteen year old boy's body. Behind her, she heard X rousing from his unconscious state, wheezing, and coughing, and gagging, as if he were choking on a mouthful of fluid, which he probably was. *Let him choke,* she thought, distantly, *let him choke and I will not have murdered him. And when he is dead, I will bury him here under this tree, and the forest can have him. Or, no,* she reconsidered. *I'll just leave him on the floor for the birds to peck at, and the foxes to eat, and they can scatter his bones so that no-one will remember him. He'll become dust, fragments, like I have. Let him rot into pieces while I put my Bobby back together again. There is justice in that.*

Her trowel hit something solid, resistant, something larger than bone fragments, but still jarringly white against the black earth. She threw the trowel to one side, and used her fingers to clean the surface of it. The object looked smooth, and round. She began to scrabble at it like a dog digging a hole, ripping great clots of soil away with her bare fingers, fingernails catching and tearing, skin snagging on tree roots and small, sharp pieces of flint. She excavated what felt like a ton of dirt in this way, and then she managed to dig her fingertips beneath the thing, feel the size and shape of it, get a purchase on it, and pull.

The soil gave up its final, gruesome secret with reluctance. Laura pulled so hard that she wasn't prepared for the sudden release, and toppled over backwards. Behind her, X groaned, but she had no mind for him, only for what came out of the earth, which, after regaining her balance, she seized in her hands, and held up reverently before her, like a priest with a chalice, only this was not the body of Christ, not the blood of the redeemer, only her friend, her Bobby, the place where his mind and his smile had once lived, where lips had been that had once kissed her, where...

She froze, staring at the thing in her hands, eyes wide with incomprehension. She saw an elongated jawbone, pointed snout, eye sockets that were in the wrong place, thick, flat, grinding teeth that jutted out from a profound under bite.

Horns.

No, not horns. Short, stubby antlers.

And then, it dawned upon her.

This was not Bobby.

This was another cruel trick.

And behind her, with a slow and rising glee, came a sound.

Laughter.

30.

Afterwards, she would tell the Police that she didn't know the gun was loaded, which was the truth. She would also tell them that the man she killed had attacked her first, which wasn't. Her statement was long, and given in several stages. Her leg had indeed become infected in the forest, and she had a prolonged hospital stay- first while they treated her body, and then while they treated her mind, which did the best it could to stay strong, but eventually, collapsed in on itself. Laura spent many days in an induced fog, painkillers and tranquilisers and mood stabilisers gradually erasing the details of her crime, but later she would find out that she had become the thing she feared the most: a murderer. X was dead, and by her hand. She was, after all that had happened, no better than he.

His real name was Stanley, Stanley Aston. He was a known sex-offender, and his name was featured on an awful lot of lists. It soon featured on an awful lot of television screens and newspapers, too, alongside a dated mugshot. Stanley, it seemed, had kept a lot of secrets with him out in the woods. And now, those secrets were unearthed, thanks to Laura.

The Police used Laura's map and letters to find Stanley's camp, and there they discovered his body, right where she had left it: splayed out on a discarded couch, a single bullet hole in his head, brain matter baked onto the faux leather beneath his skull, teeth and nose broken from her earlier, violent assault.

They found the animal remains that had been buried at the base of the tree, and forensic examination later confirmed that they belonged to a Reeves's muntjac deer.

Then, they searched Stanley's tent.

And found Bobby. Or, what was left of him, at least. His skull. Sitting on an old tapestry cushion balanced on top of a folding camp table, garlanded with a crown of ferns and moss. A large, worn, laminated photo of him was propped up behind. Candle stubs had congealed around its base in a large, molten mess.

Subsequent digging efforts around the campsite unearthed the remains of seven other adolescents, three girls and four boys. Anthropologists worked at the recovery site for months, cataloguing each bone and fragment of clothing and tiny shard of debris scattered across the site, although Laura knew little of this, swathed up as she was in her bubble-wrap world.

Seven bodies, one deer, and one young boy's head. That was the bounty of the forest, as summer turned its face to the wall, and autumn came softly in its wake.

31.

Frank, upon cross-examination, later told a courtroom filled with serious faces that he had taken up target practice at his local shooting club. He'd had his Grandfather's gun serviced especially to make it functional for this purpose, and hadn't thought to tell his wife, in case she disapproved. The jury stifled a ripple of laughter at this, the irony having not occurred to Frank until that moment.

Frank was not an experienced gun handler, and unintentionally leaving ammunition in the chamber of an antique pistol is a good way to be excommunicated from any self-respecting shooting club. Frank subsequently had to find himself a new hobby, so he took up fishing, which suited him much better. The gun remained in a Police evidence box for many years to come.

Laura was found guilty of the crime of second-degree murder. The jury did not look happy about this, and neither did the presiding judge.

'Will I go to jail?' she asked, and her lawyer nodded, patting the back of her hand sympathetically.

Laura pulled it away.

32.

Laura is much older now, and a free woman once again. She has paid for her crime, at least in the eyes of the law, and finds herself longing to undertake a pilgrimage. And so she walks through the Old Forest, her son Robert, who is now a tall, handsome replica of Frank, keeping step alongside her.

The hair that had only been speckled with grey when she'd last made this journey is now white, cropped short against her skull for the sake of ease and practicality. Her steps through the copper carpet of leaves underfoot are unsteady, but no less focused on the goal. She is headed north, to Stanley's camp, to pay her respects to Bobby. Because she's had a lot of time to think over the years, about one thing in particular. Bobby's head might now rest in a small, silk- lined cedar box in the town cemetery, but the rest of him has never been recovered. Laura knows that he is here, in this forest, the parts of him that touched and held and ran and walked in step with her now subsumed. What remained of him after Stanley separated his sweet head from his body has long since rotted, composted, fed the soil and brought new life into the world. Laura feels a small comfort at this, and hopes it will not be long before she, too, becomes part of the complex tapestry of greens and browns, of pines and larches, oaks and birches, rhododendrons and eucalyptus that reach high and thick over her head and drag their fingers through the sky. For when she dies, she wants to be burned, and scattered in this place, so she can join her friend, and they can mingle down there in the cool earth, and catch up on all that has happened since they last saw each other.

'Mum, look,' Robert murmurs suddenly, and pats her on the arm to get her attention, pointing to a patch of bracken framed with skinny young silver birch trees. There, a sturdy brown pony grazes, a white mark on its face. Beside it, a foal, paler, emblazoned with the same white patch between its eyes. Mother, and son.

Laura smiles, and closes her eyes, and absurdly, the memories that eluded her as a young girl come back in that moment, clear and unblemished, and she sees Bobby as he had been on the day he'd first kissed her, nervous, serious and pale, white-blonde hair lifting in a faint breeze.

She feels the touch of his hand on hers, as if he is standing right there next to her, instead of Robert, and she recalls his smile. The remembrance is fleeting, but crystal clear, and she is glad for it.

And now, like a little brown bird, flying north, she continues, walking on, in a straight, true line through the forest, always on, and never back, because that is not how we survive.

ABOUT THE AUTHOR

Gemma Amor is a horror fiction author from Bristol, in the UK. Her debut collection of short stories, *Cruel Works of Nature,* was published in 2018.

Gemma also writes for anthology audio dramas like the wildly popular NoSleep Podcast. She is co-creator, writer and voice actor for horror-comedy podcast Calling Darkness, and hopes to release her spooky cowboy show Whisper Ridge soon.

Her next book will be paranormal mystery novel *White Pines,* followed by another short story collection called *Till the Score is Paid.* Gemma's influences range from Carter to King, Shakespeare to Shelley, and she has a particular love for misunderstood monsters and women with an axe to grind.

gemmammorauthor.com

Facebook.com/littlescarystories
Twitter.com/manylittlewords
Instagram.com/manylittlewords

Printed in Great Britain
by Amazon